The Fisherman's Cat

written and illustrated by
CASSIE RITA AUSTIN

This book is dedicated to the family and friends of fishermen who've been lost at sea.

PAINTBRUSH TALES PUBLISHING · BEVERLY, MASSACHUSETTS

For information, contact PAINTBRUSH TALES PUBLISHING, LLC,
20 Webber Ave, Beverly, Massachusetts 01915
cassie@paintbrushtalespublishing.com

www.paintbrushtalespublishing.com

ISBN: 978-0-9846151-0-0

Book design by Adie Russell

PUBLISHER'S CATALOGING-IN-PUBLICATION DATA
(Prepared by The Donohue Group, Inc.)

Austin, Cassie Rita.
The fisherman's cat / written and illustrated by Cassie Rita Austin.

  p. : ill. ; cm.

  Summary: Jake is a very popular cat who lives in Gloucester, Massachusetts with his fisherman
owner, Captain John Blackwell. Jake's unique talent for finding fish makes the other cats jealous. When
a terrible storm leaves Jack alone at sea, he must win over the hearts of a tough gang of cats to survive.
  Interest age level: 006-010.
  ISBN: 978-0-9846151-0-0

  1. Cats — Massachusetts — Gloucester — Juvenile fiction. 2. Fishing — Massachusetts — Gloucester
— Juvenile fiction. 3. Fishing accidents — Juvenile fiction. 4. Gloucester (Mass.) — Juvenile fiction.
5. Cats — Massachusetts — Gloucester — Fiction. 6. Fishing — Massachusetts — Gloucester — Fiction.
7. Gloucester (Mass.) — Fiction. I. Title.

PZ7.A978 Fi 2010
[Fic]

Production Date: 06/29/2010
Printed by Everbest Printing Co. Ltd., Nansha, China
Job/Batch 95833

JAKE WAS A FISHERMAN'S CAT. Captain John Blackwell loved his cat so much he even named his fishing boat, "JAKE'S CATCH," after him.

The captain had no family in his seaside town of Gloucester, so he would take Jake along on all of his fishing trips. In fact, the captain and his cat spent more time together at sea than they ever did on land.

The captain was very serious and very strict about his fishing business. He expected the entire crew to work hard, including Jake.

On land, Jake could be a regular playful and carefree cat, but at sea there was no room for any nonsense. Jake had to learn to be a good shipmate and he was required to do chores.

"Good fishing," the captain would say,
                              "requires good teamwork."

Jake would help to load and unload fishing equipment.

Jake would also help recoil ropes that were used for many fishing tasks such as securing the boat to the moorings, tying to buoys and anchors or to use as a heaving line to an approaching vessel.

"The ropes," Captain Blackwell taught Jake, *"could also save lives.* It is important to keep them well-coiled and handy for an emergency."

Sometimes Jake would climb the tallest mast, to use it as a lookout,

and warn the crew of any dangers that might lie ahead in the waters.

But the captain's cat also served a very unique purpose.
Call it cat's intuition if you will, for Jake had this uncanny
ability to guide the boat directly to where schools of
fish gathered.

With a leftward gesture of his paw, Jake would direct
the captain to turn the boat to its left side, which
fishermen refer to as the *"port side"* of the boat.

When Jake wanted to turn the boat to the right,
his paw faced the *"starboard side"* of the boat.

Both paws crossed would signal the captain that they were
in the area of the fish.

The crew would refer to Jake's find as the
"mother lode."

"Jake found the mother lode again!"
the crew would shout as they pulled up
their nets and lines, filling them with fish
over
and over
again.

They would then store their catch on ice in the lower deck, or hull, in a compartment called the "hold." The fish would chill in the hold until the crew returned to mainland.

Business was good for Captain John Blackwell and his crew. Thanks to Jake, their lucky fish finder, the fish sales provided them all with a good living.

It provided Jake with a good living, too!

After every big catch, Jake was rewarded with an

"all-you-can-eat-fish-buffet,"

which he ate right out of a bucket the fishermen filled for him.

It was making him immensely plump and he often ate

so much he got sick.

That didn't stop
him, though, from
looking forward to
the next feast.

When JAKE'S CATCH returned to shore, the captain
would pull the boat up to the fish-processing
warehouse to offload the fish before
docking in their usual slip.

The crew was so happy with Jake's success at finding the
mother lode that they spoiled him with extra attention
and affection in between fishing trips on the Rocky Neck
shore of Gloucester's harbor.

It was something the other
cats took notice to.

Jake felt so full of himself he would often show off by acting goofy to entertain the crew. Sometimes he would wear a fisherman's hat while dancing the

"Cha-cha-cha..."

…or act like a clown walking on his front paws while
hula-hooping a life buoy around his waist.
The other Gloucester cats felt Jake did this purposefully
to make them more envious of his privileged life.

The Rudder Restaurant was a favorite meeting place for the fishermen and Jake was allowed to go there with them. He was passed from lap to lap and fed fresh clam plates and bowls of milk right on top of the bar counter. No other cat was allowed inside The Rudder let alone to climb *on its countertops!*

When the other Gloucester cats caught wind of this, the fur on their arched backs spiked like a porcupine. They became so jealous of Jake that it was dangerous for him to roam the streets alone at night.

The fisherman's cat had one such encounter that nearly cost him *his life.*

Jake stepped out of the restaurant by himself one evening and walked into a small alley between The Rudder Restaurant and The Mad Fish Grille. A group of cats, known as the *Rudder Alley Cats,* boxed him in from both ends of the alley, but Jake's swift ability to climb masts in terrible storms saved his life. He shimmied his way up a support beam and made his way up to the roof and then off the other side of the building to freedom.

From that time on, Jake stuck with the fishermen

and never strayed off alone.

Captain Blackwell, Jake and the crew ventured out for another trip one Friday in late August that began in good spirit and good weather. But Fridays were considered to be "bad luck days" by many fishermen who declined to take such a chance. Captain Blackwell dismissed such superstitious nonsense and knew that his ship always had luck on its side.

"Green luck," the captain would say referring to the ship's rich color, *"like leprechauns' eyes."*

JAKE'S CATCH faded from the mainland into a tiny speck of green.

"Steady as she goes," the captain proudly exclaimed from the helm of his old faithful ship, which held a steady course over a calm sea. But their fate would soon change. JAKE'S CATCH would soon encounter its greatest challenge.

The fisherman's cat was good with fish intuition but he had no intuition whatsoever for predicting weather. Soon, dark clouds crept into the sky like sneaky ghosts as the ocean became hauntingly restless. As usual, Jake directed the crew to the mother lode of fish but directly into the *eye of a storm.*

"Shiver me timbers!" cried the captain when

a massive thirty-foot wave emerged from the stormy sea.

Natures force overpowered JAKE'S CATCH and the entire
crew went down with the boat, except Jake.

He clung tightly to the top of the mast, which managed to
remain above water until the storm ceased. A life buoy passed
by Jake, as if it was waiting for him, and he jumped onto it.

Jake drifted swiftly away from the mast, now the size of a
pin in its distance. JAKE'S CATCH would never return to the
shores of Gloucester.

Jake was cold, tired and scared after drifting for hours at sea by himself.

He kept scanning his surroundings for the rest of the crew hoping that somehow they survived. He longed to return to the harbor and back to shore but knew it would not be safe for him amongst those jealous Rudder Alley Cats.

So he stopped his floating device before the Rocky Neck shore
    to a small island in the harbor only reachable by boat,
        unless you were *a very good swimmer.*

His new home would be the

Ten Pound Island Lighthouse.

Jake pulled the floating device up close to the edge of the tiny island
and jumped onto a rock. He shook the salty water off his thick fur
and took a nap in the soft, grassy area at the base of the lighthouse.

He woke the following morning to a swarm of seagulls clamoring above him. At first he had no idea know where he was, like waking up from a crazy dream and taking a moment or two to realize that you're home in your own bed. Only Jake wasn't waking up where he usually did, in Captain Blackwell's house or the lower deck of JAKE'S CATCH in the sleeping quarters.

Jake knew he wasn't in either of those places.

Sometimes he would take naps on the upper deck on long fishing journeys while the crew chit-chatted and played cards to pass time.

He knew he wasn't waking up there either.

The long blades of grass felt prickly against his face. Jake shook his head back and forth as the grass blades seemed to sword fight with his own whiskers.

When he looked up at the tall lighthouse he closed his eyes tight and reopened them quickly hoping it would change to the tall mast of the ship. But it didn't. Jake remembered why he was here on the island and he didn't like that memory at all. Everything happened so quickly in that terrible storm.

The sea took away the only life he knew.

What would he do now?

The fisherman's cat spent most of his time at
the top of the lighthouse tower on the lookout,
like he did on the mast of JAKE'S CATCH.
He kept thinking that one day he'd see Captain
John Blackwell or other crewmembers that
may have survived the storm. Perhaps they
drifted off to a distant island and would
return home one day.

When he got hungry, Jake would climb down the lighthouse and catch
a fish or two using his intuition and catching techniques he learned
from the crew.

Sometimes he enjoyed a *"surf and turf"* meal by catching
rodents on the island after his fish catch.

When Jake was thirsty, he drank rainwater that
formed *puddles* at the top of the lighthouse.

From the main shores of Gloucester, rumors spread about the
cat that lived in the lighthouse on Ten Pound Island and they all
believed it was Jake, *the lucky fish finder*.

Other fishermen would tell tales of a cat who would climb onto their
boat as they passed by the lighthouse and guide them to a mother lode
of fish. After being rewarded with his "all-you-can-eat-fish-buffet,"
he would then jump off the boat at the end of their trip and return to
the lighthouse.

But Jake's purpose for venturing frequently out to sea had little
to do with helping the fishermen and eating his buffet.
Each venture brought hope in finding and rescuing
Captain John Blackwell and the crew.

Sometimes at night Jake would peek inland and see shadows of cat figures walking the shore of Rocky Neck and chasing seagulls off the pier. The Rudder Alley Cats would sometimes look out at the flickering red light from the lighthouse and see the shadow of a familiar, plump-bellied cat. *Their glowing eyes* seemed to fixate on Jake like they did that night when they wanted to attack him in Rudder Alley

The tension between Jake and the Rudder Alley Cats troubled Jake very much and he wondered why they still bothered with him when he had nothing left to be jealous of. Perhaps he used to be spoiled by Captain John Blackwell and his crew, and, yes, maybe he did live a privileged life with his restaurant eating and all the attention from the crew. Was that any reason for those cats to dislike Jake so much now?

Perhaps yes, perhaps no.

Jake thought about how Captain Blackwell used to deal with unfriendly fishermen he'd cross at sea. Usually they, too, were jealous because JAKE'S CATCH always managed to find fish even on days when every other fishing vessel had no luck. Captain Blackwell would approach those bitter fishermen and offer them the coordinates to the mother lode. Sometimes, he would even share half his catch if they were really down on their luck.

"*Enemies,*" the captain would tell Jake, "find it nearly impossible
to continue being mean to you if you're always kind in return.

That is the golden secret of turning enemies *into friends.*"

Jake had an idea.

On the next fishing trip, he boarded the "SHIP'S A-JOY"
skippered by *Captain Linda* and her crew of four.

After Jake led them to the mother lode,
he set aside his "all-you-can-eat-fish-buffet" throwing extra fish
into the bucket he usually feasted out of. Before he went his own separate
way to the lighthouse, Jake asked the crew if they would kindly drop his
bucket of fish off to his friends in Rudder Alley.

"Compliments of the lighthouse cat," said one
of the fishermen to the Rudder Alley Cats who
hesitated in a moment of shock before
devouring the fish.

From that day on,
after every fishing trip,
the Rudder Alley Cats would be greeted by another complimentary fish
feast from the lighthouse cat. They would look forward to those fish feasts
and they were all growing very plump bellies just like Jake.

Those once frightening, enemy eyes turned into happy, friendly eyes and
sometimes Jake would see those Gloucester street cats making gestures
with their paws as if they were inviting him back to the mainland.

"I can't go back," Jake thought,
     "I've got to keep watching."

Then he turned to the direction of the vast open sea looking out, as he often did, for Captain John Blackwell and
his crew. It was too soon for the fisherman's cat to give up
hope, too soon to give up his post on the lighthouse.

Jake took a deep breath. He could smell the fish in the
salty sea and it made him hungry. "I've got everything
I need here," thought Jake, "Even though I'm lonely."

And lonely he was. He thought about how good life
     was aboard JAKE'S CATCH.

It was the love and
comfort of his crew that
he missed so much. It
was that love that made
him feel so big.

He felt so little now.

Jake thought about the *Gloucester Fisherman Memorial*
statue that Captain Blackwell took him to one time after
one of his friends died on a stormy fishing trip. The statue
was a symbol of both pride and pain for the families of
fishermen who'd been lost at sea. Jake didn't want to feel
that kind of pride nor that pain. He shut that thought out
of his mind and held onto his hope.

In the late fall it became increasingly difficult to live on the island when the wind from the cooling sea chilled the fisherman's cat to the bone. It was even colder inside the lighthouse as the dark, enclosed cement structure was much like a damp basement only worsened by the fact that there was no warm house above to provide some secondary heat. Jake could find no warm spot on the island but at least the top of the lighthouse brought him closer to the sun.

He caught fewer fish these days as he grew more reluctant to descend the lighthouse and soak his fur in the frigid water. The rodents appeared to be hibernating so his hunt on land grew scarce, too. Fishing ventures were few and far between as the approaching winter slowed business for the season. Needless to say, the plump fisherman's cat was getting quite lean.

Jake would often fall in and out of sleep, dazed and confused between the life in his dreams and his terrifying real-life circumstances. He was growing weaker and leaner and lonelier with each passing day. In a crazy dream one day, Jake imagined that he was back in the midst of that terrible storm. He stood up on the life buoy, just like a cowboy, with a neatly coiled rope in hand. He lassoed the rope around each of the crew and pulled them onto his life buoy one by one. Then into the sunset they drifted, all making it safely to shore.

Jake woke from his dream with an alarming question.

Where was the rope when he needed it the most?

Jake remembered Captain Blackwell's words,

"The ropes could save lives… always keep

them well-coiled and handy."

The little fisherman's cat forced himself to stay awake as much as possible

during the day to avoid such frightening dreams and troubling questions.

Shivering from the top of
the lighthouse one day in early
December, as he desperately watched
for the crew of JAKE'S CATCH, he saw a boat
from the mainland approaching his island. As
the boat drew near, Jake could see it was Captain
Linda and crew on the SHIP'S-A-JOY. This time,
however, Jake counted six additional crewmembers.

As the boat moored to a rock on the island, Jake feebly attempted to descend the lighthouse to greet his guests. He figured he would just send them on their way, as he had grown too weak for fishing ventures.

But the once invincible fisherman's cat was barely able to take a single step before collapsing on his tail. Suddenly he was clinging to the top of the lighthouse like he clung to the top of the mast of JAKE'S CATCH during the storm. This time, however, there was no life buoy waiting to save him.

In his half-alert state of mind, Jake could hear footsteps climbing up the lighthouse.

Then there before him stood
the six additional crewmembers.

It was the Rudder Alley cats. Jake was surprised to see them and had no idea of their intentions. His mind flashed back to that dreadful night in Rudder Alley and he thought he was about to be attacked again. Jake was too weak to defend himself and, so,

he simply fainted.

When Jake woke, he was lying in Rudder Alley surrounded by the
Rudder Alley Cats and a bucket of fish. He could taste milk on his lips
that someone must have fed him while he was unconscious.

"What am I doing here?" said Jake.

"We rescued you, slim," said one of the cats,
"Now eat up. I'm getting hungry just looking at you!"

Jake smiled. He could feel the warmth of love returning in his blood
with the comfort of his new friends. He was thankful they saved his life.
The Rudder Alley Cats were his life buoy. He thought about the first time
he sent them a bucket of fish. He was thankful he did that now.

Jake adjusted well to his new life, hanging with his friends in the alley, eating discarded leftovers from the restaurants, and his occasional ventures to sea to bring home the fish feasts for all to share.

Before long, the fisherman's cat was back to his old jovial self, feeling big again and entertaining his friends in Rudder Alley. He was happy and no longer lonely.

But from time to time he still looked out to sea, thinking about Captain Blackwell and crew and hoping they would return home one day on Jake's Catch.

❧ The End ❧